A Note to Parents

DK READERS is a compelling program for beginning readers, designed in conjunction with leading literacy experts, including Dr. Linda Gambrell, Professor of Education at Clemson University. Dr. Gambrell has served as President of the International Reading Association, National Reading Conference, and College Reading Association.

Beautiful illustrations and superb full-color photographs combine with engaging, easy-to-read stories and informational texts to offer a fresh approach to each subject in the series. Each DK READER is guaranteed to capture a child's interest while developing his or her reading skills, general knowledge, and love of reading.

The five levels of DK READERS are aimed at different reading abilities, enabling you to choose the books that are exactly right for your child:

Pre-level 1: Learning to read

Level 1: Beginning to read

Level 2: Beginning to read alone

Level 3: Reading alone

Level 4: Proficient readers

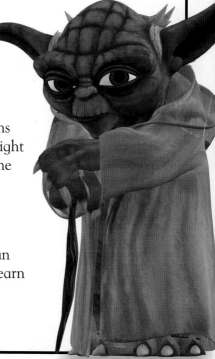

The "normal" age at which a child begins to read can be anywhere from three to eight years old. Adult participation through the lower levels is very helpful for providing encouragement, discussing storylines, and sounding out unfamiliar words.

No matter which level you select, you can be sure that you are helping your child learn to read, then read to learn!

LONDON, NEW YORK, MUNICH,
MELBOURNE, AND DELHI

For Dorling Kindersley
Project Editor Heather Scott
Designer John DeGray
Senior Designer Ron Stobbart
Brand Manager Lisa Lanzarini
Publishing Manager Simon Beecroft
Category Publisher Alex Allan
Production Controller Jen Lockwood
Production Editor Sean Daly

For Lucasfilm
Executive Editor Jonathan W. Rinzler
Art Director Troy Alders
Keeper of the Holocron Leland Chee
Director of Publishing Carol Roeder

Reading Consultant
Linda B. Gambrell, Ph.D.

First published in the United States in 2009 by
DK Publishing
375 Hudson Street
New York, New York, 10014

10 11 12 13 10 9 8 7 6
CD295—12/08

DK Books are available at special discounts when purchased in bulk for
sales promotions, premiums, fund-raising, or educational use.
For details, contact: DK Publishing Special Markets, 375 Hudson
Street, New York, New York 10014
SpecialSales@dk.com

Published in Great Britain by Dorling Kindersley Limited.

A catalog record for this book
is available from the Library of Congress.

ISBN: 978-0-7566-4515-1 (Hardcover)
ISBN: 978-0-7566-4514-4 (Paperback)

Color reproduction by Alta Image, UK
Printed and bound by L-Rex, China

Discover more at
www.dk.com
www.starwars.com

STAR WARS®

THE CLONE WARS™

WITHDRAWN

Yoda
In Action!

Written by Heather Scott

Jedi Master Yoda is going to a lonely
moon called Rugosa in his ship. He is
meeting the King of the Toydarians, King
Katuunko. The Republic wants to make
a treaty with the Toydarians, so they can
build a base in the Toydarian star system.
"Toydarian Royal Delegation, this is
the Republic Envoy. Please respond.
Toydarian Delegation, please respond,"
says Captain Zak into the computer.
Static buzzes over the computer.

King Katuunko

King Katuunko is the King of the
Toydarians. Toydarians are an
alien species that has small wings.
They can hover in the air.

King Katuunko has landed on Rugosa
and looks for Yoda through his
binoculars. He can't see anything.

"We're getting no signal from the
Republic, Your Highness," says one of
the King's guards.

"It is not like the Jedi to be late," King Katuunko says to his guards.

"Greetings, King Katuunko," says a mysterious hooded figure.

"Who are you?" demands the King.

The figure lowers her hood to reveal a white face and cold eyes. It's Asajj Ventress—the deadly assassin!

Ventress lowers a holoprojector to the ground, and a hologram of Count Dooku appears. Count Dooku wants the King to join the Separatists.

Asajj Ventress
Ventress used to be a Jedi. She turned to the dark side after her Jedi Master was killed. She fights with twin red lightsabers.

He says that the Separatist Army is much bigger and will beat the Republic's army. King Katuunko is not sure. Count Dooku orders his ships to attack Yoda's ship to prove his point.

Yoda and his clone troopers are rocked by the sudden explosions. Another one of Count Dooku's ships appears and fires on Yoda's ship, too. Yoda realizes that it is too late to escape in his ship. Yoda must still get down to the moon's surface if he is to meet the King.

"Quickly now. Reach the moon's surface we must," urges Yoda.

"In a life pod, sir? The enemy will fire at anything we launch," says Captain Zak.

"Then launch all of them you will. Hmm?" Yoda suggests.

The life pods launch and the enemy ships fire at them.

Life Pod
Yoda escapes in a life pod with Lieutenant Thire and clone troopers Jjeck and Rys. They head toward the moon's surface.

"Master Yoda's powers have been greatly exaggerated," Dooku says.

"That remains to be seen, Count," replies King Katuunko.

"Indeed. When you decide to join us, my apprentice will contact me," says Dooku as he bows and fades out.

"My Lord, Master Yoda's warship has fled the system. What further evidence do you require of the Jedi's weakness?" asks Ventress.

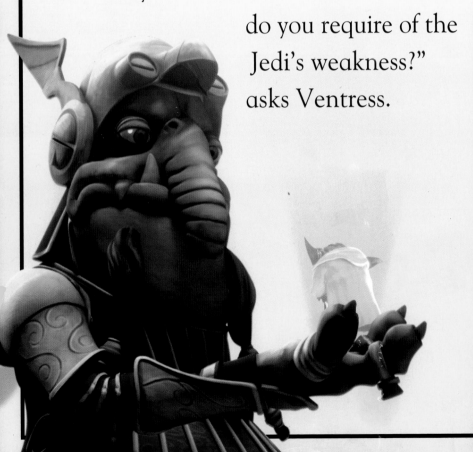

King Katuunko's holoprojector lights up.
Yoda greets the King and tells him that
he will still be able to come and meet
him. Ventress interrupts.

"Allow me to send my best troops to
capture him. If he escapes, join the
Republic. But should my droids defeat
Yoda, consider an alliance with the
Separatists," Ventress sneers.

"Accept the challenge I do, Your
Highness. Arrive by nightfall, I will,"
Yoda promises.

Yoda and King Katuunko are to meet at a distant coral tree. A Separatist ship lands on the moon, right between Yoda and the coral tree.

"Carry only what you need. Too much weight, slow you down it will. Destroy Ventress, your weapons will not," Yoda tells his clone troopers.

Lieutenant Thire points to the coral tree. "Sir, the meeting point is that way."

Ancient Moon
Rugosa has many ancient corals because it was once covered by huge oceans, which later dried up.

"As is our enemy. To reach our goal, a straight path we will not follow," Yoda says wisely.

Yoda leads his troops toward a thick coral forest nearby. The droid army marches toward the coral forest, too.

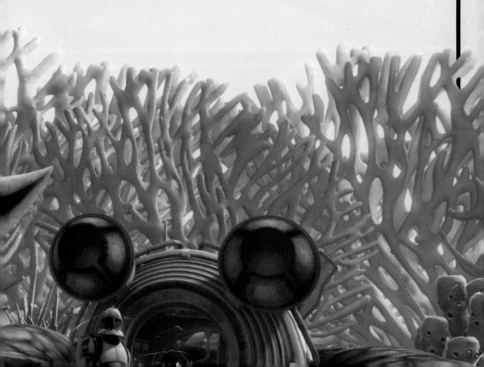

The droid tanks are too big to fit
into the coral forest. So the droids march
into the forest on foot.

"Size is not everything, mmm?
Smaller in number we are, but larger in
mind," Yoda chuckles.

"Do you have any idea
what the General is talking
about?" asks Rys.

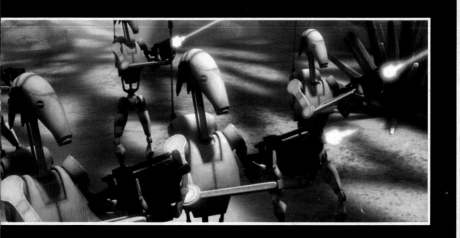

"How should I know? There's no figuring a Jedi Master," answers Jjeck.

Thire decides that they can attack the droids from the side. Yoda heads off in the other direction. A squad of Battle Droids walks past Jjeck who is hiding behind some coral. He blasts the head off of the lead droid. The other droids spot Jjeck and fire, as he turns and runs for cover.

A squad of Battle Droids sees Yoda, so they fire at him—but he jumps quickly on top of the coral and out of sight.

Suddenly, Yoda drops onto one of the droid's shoulders. The other droids aim and fire, but Yoda jumps away as the laser fire blows off the droid's head.

Yoda leaps from head to head, while the droids blast each other to pieces.

The three clones are outnumbered by a quad of Super Battle Droids, so they retreat into the forest.

Squads of Super Battle Droids swarm into the coral forest after the clones. One of the Super Battle Droids fires a rocket which explodes, sending Thire flying into the coral and injuring his leg.

Yoda leaps in front of the clones and deflects the droids' laser fire with his lightsaber. The laser bolts hit some of the droids, but more of them are surging up from behind. Yoda and the clones are trapped. Yoda closes his eyes and meditates. As the Super Battle Droids march in, Yoda calmly raises his hand.

One droid lifts off the ground, and continues to walk and fire in mid-air. Yoda waves his hand, and the droid spins around

and fires on his squad.

The droid doesn't know what is happening.

"Don't shoot! I'm on your side," shouts the confused droid, but the other droids shoot back at him. Yoda sends the droid flying into the remaining droids, destroying them. They have been defeated!

Yoda and the clones hear the sound of rolling metal.

"Rollies, inbound!"

Three Destroyer Droids roll into view, unfold, and open fire on Yoda and the clone troopers.

Destroyer Droids
Destroyer Droids, also called droidekas, can roll into a ball and travel along the ground. They can also activate a defense shield around themselves.

"Retreat! Cover you, I will!" shouts Yoda, jumping onto Rys's back as the clones run as quickly as they can. Yoda deflects a couple of blasts into a column of coral and it falls like a giant tree to block the Destroyers' path!

"The Republic troops are injured. The Jedi is in full retreat, Supreme Leader," reports a droid commander to Ventress.

"Good, pursue them without delay," replies Ventress.

"The contest is not over yet," says King Katuunko.

The King contacts Yoda on his holoprojector.

"Master Yoda! I hear you're having trouble with the droid army?" asks the King.

"Trouble? I know nothing of this trouble. Look forward to our meeting soon, I do," replies Yoda.

The King's holoprojector flies from his hand into Ventress's grasp. She furiously crushes it.

"The Jedi won't elude me for long," she snarls.

Yoda leads the clone troopers into a cave in a narrow canyon to rest. The droid tanks batter down the forest as they pursue Yoda. The clones are tired. They spread out their few remaining weapons on the floor.

Yoda takes the two damaged rifles and puts one on top of the other to make a crutch for Thire.

"So certain of defeat are you, mmm?" asks Yoda, welding the two rifles together with his lightsaber.

"Come, sit. Your helmets. Remove them. Your faces I wish to see," says Yoda.

Clone Army
The Republic's army is made up of soldiers called clone troopers who all look the same.

Yoda tells the clones they are all different, even though they share the same face.

"Clones you may be, but the Force resides in all life-forms. Use it you can, to quiet your mind," Yoda advises.

Three tanks roll into the narrow canyon. A squad of Battle Droids rides on the outside of each tank. Destroyer Droids roll alongside them.

"Greet them I will," Yoda says.

"General, you don't plan to take on the whole column by yourself?" Lieutenant Thire asks.

"Have you three, I do! Outnumbered are they. Know the time to help me, you will," Yoda chuckles.

The droid tanks continue to roll into the canyon; the lead tank slows to a standstill. There's something in the way. It's Yoda!

"It's the Jedi! Block his escape!" the droid commander instructs. "Prepare to fire!"

Yoda darts under the first tank just in time to avoid its fire. When the smoke clears, he has vanished from the droids' sight. Yoda uses his lightsaber to cut a hole in the tank's belly. He climbs up inside the tank.

There is a sound of clanking and fighting from inside the tank.

The back of the tank opens and two
droids come running out, trying to get
away. Yoda Force-pulls the droids back
into the tank. An annoyed Battle Droid
commander peers down into the hatch
and is sliced into several pieces by Yoda's
quick blade. Yoda leaps from the top of
the tank onto the droids' heads, slicing
them up as he goes.

Yoda lands in front of the barrel
of the second tank. The tank
commander sees Yoda—he's
right in their line of fire.
"We've got him in
our sights!"
Yoda leaps into the
air just as the tank
fires. The blast hits
the first tank and
destroys it.
Yoda comes down
and scrambles up the
barrel and onto the top
of the tank. He cuts a hole
in its top and Force-pulls the
Battle Droid tank driver out
and sends him flying into the air.

King Katuunko hovers at the edge
of the tree, flanked by Royal Guards.
Black smoke curls up into the sky
from the battle.

"That's a lot of smoke for a
surrender…" the King chuckles.

Ventress turns away secretively and
activates her holoprojector to speak to
the droid commander.

"Where is two-two-four?" she demands.

"Destroyed, Supreme Leader. The Jedi has overrun our position, agAHH!" Yoda leaps into the hologram and slashes apart the Battle Droid. Ventress seethes with cold fury.

"I think all those stories about the Jedi are true," says the King, looking over Ventress's shoulder.

"The fight isn't over yet, Majesty," replies Ventress coolly, activating a control that sends another squad of Destroyer Droids rolling into the forest.

The last droid collapses into a heap, destroyed by Yoda. The clones watch, amazed at Yoda's victory.

Jjeck spots the Destroyer Droids— approaching the battle at high speed.

"We got trouble."

"The clankers sent reinforcements," says Thire grimly. "The General's too busy with that tank. He won't see 'em coming."

"I think I know how to deal with them," says Thire, hatching a plan.

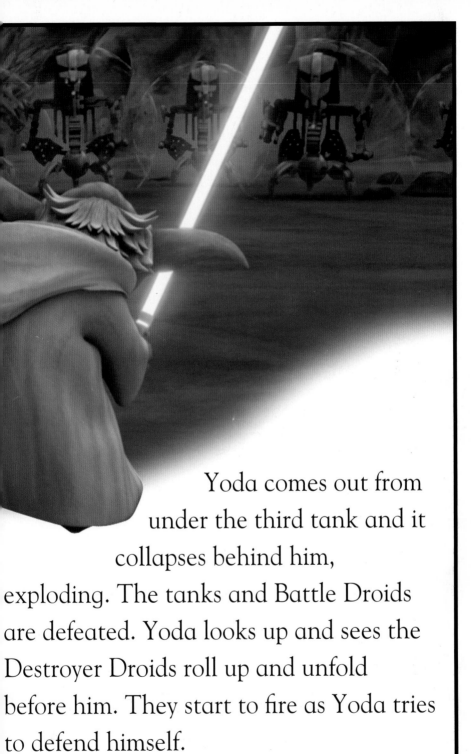

Yoda comes out from under the third tank and it collapses behind him, exploding. The tanks and Battle Droids are defeated. Yoda looks up and sees the Destroyer Droids roll up and unfold before him. They start to fire as Yoda tries to defend himself.

Thire fires his rocket at a huge piece of coral that hangs over the Destroyer Droids. The coral breaks and a large chunk tumbles down onto the Destroyer Droids below, crushing them.
Yoda is saved!

The three clones limp out to join Yoda standing peacefully among smoke and droid rubble.

Yoda holds out his finger as a baby nebray flutters down to perch on it.

"Hmmm. Learned something today have you, Lieutenant? Hmm?" Yoda asks.

"I think we all did, General," replies Thire.

"Come, behind schedule are we. Not polite to be late," says Yoda as he hurries off.

"You were right, Count Dooku, one Jedi is not worth a hundred Battle Droids. More like a thousand! I'm sorry, but I will be joining the Republic," says King Katuunko to a hologram of Count Dooku.

"I urge you to reconsider, wise King. I promise you won't regret it," replies Dooku.

"Your agent also promised me Yoda would get a fair fight. I will not deal with those who break their words."

"So be it. Perhaps our negotiations will
be more fruitful with your successor.
Ventress! Kill him!" orders Count Dooku.

Ventress raises her crimson blades
ready to strike the King, when she
suddenly freezes in midair. She looks
around, confused to see
Yoda using the Force to
hold her frozen.

Nearby Battle Droids turn to shoot, but the clones quickly blast them to the ground.

"Jedi Master Yoda! I am very pleased to meet you, at last!" the King says.

Yoda bows and says, "Share the feeling I do, King Katuunko."

Yoda pushes Ventress along the ground, sliding her away from the King.

Yoda raises his hand and Ventress's lightsabers are yanked out of her hands. They deactivate and fly

through the air into Yoda's hands. He examines them.

"Still much to learn you have." He tosses the lightsabers back to her. "Surrender you should."

Ventress realizes that she doesn't stand a chance against Yoda. She puts her lightsabers back into her belt, at the same time pressing a button. On the cliff above, the King's ship explodes with a tremendous boom. Rubble rains down toward Yoda and King Katuunko.

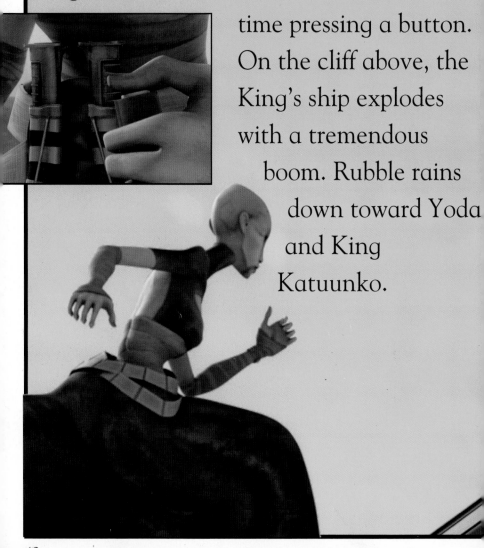

Yoda raises his hand and stops the rubble falling on them as Ventress takes her chance to escape. When Yoda looks up, Ventress is already in her ship and taking off.

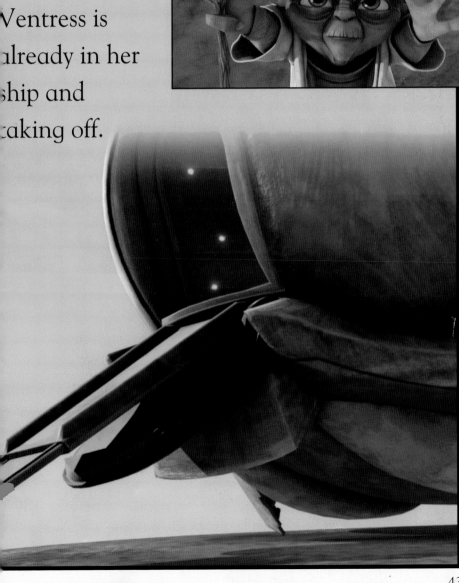

"Hmph. In the end, cowards are those who follow the dark side," Yoda says.

"It's a pity I wasn't there in person, my old Master," says Dooku, from the holoprojector.

"A pity indeed, my fallen apprentice," replies Yoda.

The hologram fizzles out.
"Perhaps now, begin
negotiations we can,"
Yoda suggests to the King.
"That is not necessary,

my friend. You have my faith. Toydaria
would be honored to host a Republic base.
My people are at your service," replies
the King.

The King presents a decorated sword to Yoda, a Toydarian sign of respect.

Yoda bows and takes the sword. Yoda looks to his clones to say thanks.

"Your Majesty, fail you, we will not," Yoda promises.

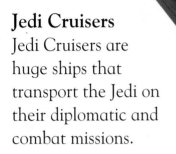

Jedi Cruisers
Jedi Cruisers are huge ships that transport the Jedi on their diplomatic and combat missions.

The Republic ships reappear in the sky, with two Jedi Cruisers. One of the ships lands on the moon, while the others circle the area on the look out for Separatist ships. Yoda and the King enter the ship with the clone troopers. It lifts off and flies to the Jedi Cruisers above.

Glossary

A

alliance
ah-LIE-ence
An association between two groups to help each other.

apprentice
ap-PREN-tis
Someone who is learning a skill from their master.

assassin
ah-SASS-in
A person who is paid to kill people.

D

delegation
del-ee-GAY-shun
A group of people chosen to represent others.

E

envoy
EN-voy
A diplomatic representative.

F

Force, the
A mystical energy that Jedi believe is in all living things.

H

hologram
HOL-o-gram
A three-dimensional image of a person or thing.

holoprojector
HOL-o-pro-JECT-er
A device that displays moving holograms.

J

Jedi
JED-eye
A person who has been trained in the Jedi arts and has sworn to protect the Republic.

L

lightsaber
light-SABE-er
A weapon, like a sword, that can cut through almost everything.

M

meditation
med-ee-TAY-shun
To focus or concentrate the mind.

N

Nebray
NEB-ray
A birdlike creature that grows to a huge size.

R

republic
REE-pub-lick
A state whose head is not a king or queen and whose power belongs to the people.

S

separatists
SEP-prah-tists
A group of people that want to break away from the rule of the current system.

T

treaty
TREE-tee
An agreement made by two countries or nations, often as a signed document.